Disney
PRINCESS

Jasmine
The Jewel Orchard

By Ellie O'Ryan
Illustrated by
the Disney Storybook Artists

DISNEP PRESS
New York

visit us at www.abdopublishing.com

Reinforced library bound edition published in 2014 by Spotlight, a division of the
ABDO Group, PO Box 398166, Minneapolis, MN 55439. Spotlight produces high-
quality reinforced library bound editions for schools and libraries. Published by
agreement with Disney Press.

Printed in the United States of America, North Mankato, Minnesota.
102013
012014
 This book contains at least 10% recycled materials.

Library of Congress Cataloging-in-Publication Data
This title was previously cataloged with the following information:
O'Ryan, Ellie.
 Jasmine : the jewel orchard / by Ellie O'Ryan ; illustrated by the Disney Storybook
Artists.
 p. cm. -- (Disney Princess)
 Summary: One morning at the palace, Jasmine overhears a surprising
conversation. A servant claims that there is no fruit to be found in all of Agrabah!
Jasmine heads to the market to figure out what has happened. When a trail of
beautiful amethysts leads her to the royal orchards, she discovers that all the fruit
and water have been turned into sparkling, shimmering jewels! At first it seems a
beautiful sight, but with no fruit to eat or water to drink, the people of Agrabah can't
survive. Jasmine and Aladdin must figure out how to reverse the spell that has been
cast upon the orchards before it's too late.
 1. Aladdin (Legendary character)--Juvenile fiction. 2. Princesses--Juvenile fiction.
3. Jinn--Juvenile fiction. 4. Magic--Juvenile fiction. I. Title. II Series.
 PZ7.O78417 Jas 2013
 [Fic]--dc23   2012942011

ISBN 978-1-61479-213-0 (Reinforced Library Bound Edition)

spotlight

All Spotlight books are reinforced library binding
and manufactured in the United States of America.

Chapter One

The moment Princess Jasmine walked into the palace dining room, she could tell something was wrong. Her father, the Sultan of Agrabah, had a huge frown on his face, and there was nothing on his breakfast plate. *That* was unusual.

"Good morning, Father," Jasmine said as she slipped into her usual seat. She reached for a crystal pitcher and poured herself a glass of milk. "Is everything all right?"

"Well, my dear, not really," the Sultan said, clearly distressed. He gestured at the table.

Jasmine glanced at all the food. She saw platters of pastries and bowls of creamy yogurt topped with honey and walnuts. In the center of the table was a tower of breads and hot rolls. It looked like a feast fit for a sultan!

"I think everything looks delicious!" Jasmine replied.

The Sultan looked disappointed. "Where are my favorite date-and-apple pancakes?" he asked.

Jasmine tried not to smile. "Oh, I *do*

see that those are missing," she said sympathetically. She looked at one of the servers. "Rajeed, did something happen to the pancakes?"

Rajeed took a step forward. "Princess, please accept the apologies of the kitchen. The royal chef was unable to prepare the pancakes, as there were no dates to be had in the market."

"Thank you, Rajeed," Jasmine said kindly. Then she turned to the Sultan. "I knew there had to be a reasonable explanation."

"I suppose," the Sultan said, still pouting. "Rajeed, would you please tell the chef that I would love some persimmon soup with lunch?"

"We will do our very best," Rajeed

promised before he left the dining room.

"It just doesn't make any sense," the Sultan said to his daughter. "This is the height of date season! How can the entire market of Agrabah run out of dates?"

"Well, perhaps you're not the only one who is so fond of date-and-apple pancakes," Jasmine teased her father. "And I'm sure that your special pancakes will be served as soon as more dates have been harvested."

"Very well." The Sultan sighed. Then he glanced around the table and realized that someone was missing: Prince Aladdin, Jasmine's husband. "Where is Aladdin this morning?"

"Oh, he and the Magic Carpet left before

dawn," Jasmine replied. "They're on their way to the royal menagerie. The peacock hatchlings are big enough to live in the pavilion now!"

For the first time that morning, the Sultan smiled. "Splendid, splendid!" he exclaimed. For weeks, the Sultan had been looking forward to the peacocks' arrival. He loved the birds' brilliantly colored feathers. "And what will you do today, dearest?" he asked his daughter.

"Oh, I'm sure I'll think of something," replied Jasmine. She glanced across the table at Aladdin's pet monkey, Abu, who had stuffed his face with walnuts. "Abu, maybe you'd like to help me get the pavilion ready for the peacocks."

Abu clapped his hands as he jumped up
and down, scattering broken walnut shells
across the table.

As soon as they finished breakfast,
Jasmine and Abu went to the pavilion.
Jasmine could hardly believe what she saw
there. The fresh straw for the peacocks' nests
had been scattered throughout the open
courtyard. One of the tall fountains had

been knocked over. There were even some tiles that had fallen off the roof!

"This is dreadful!" Jasmine gasped. "What happened here?"

"It was the storm, Princess!" a servant called from the roof. "All that wind last night caused more damage than we expected. But we'll have it fixed in no time."

"Oh, yes," Jasmine said at once. "That was a tremendous windstorm, wasn't it? Well, don't worry about the peacock area. Abu and I will take care of that."

First, Jasmine and Abu made sure that the peacocks' nests were full of fresh, clean straw. Then Jasmine moved the nests closer to a fountain so that the peacocks would have plenty of water to drink.

Abu started chattering as he pointed at a large bowl near the fountain.

"You're absolutely right, Abu," Jasmine said. "Our peacocks will need some grain, of course! I will go and get some from the kitchen."

That made Abu chatter even louder—and this time, he rubbed his tummy.

Jasmine laughed. "Are you hungry, too? I will bring you a snack. Would you like some grapes?"

Abu grinned and nodded his head. He never turned down a snack!

"I'll be right back," Jasmine promised. She picked up the bowl and carried it to the kitchen. As she poured the grain for the peacocks, Jasmine couldn't help overhearing

a conversation between Rajeed and the royal chef.

"And I am telling *you* that it is not possible!" the chef cried.

"Then perhaps *you* should be the one to explain that to His Majesty, the Sultan," Rajeed replied. "He has requested persimmon soup for lunch, and I am merely passing on his request."

"But how can I make persimmon soup without persimmons?" the chef cried. "I am not a miracle worker! How can I make something out of nothing!"

"Perhaps the fruit deliveries were late this morning," Rajeed suggested.

The chef shook his head. "Amir just came back from the market," he said. "I told him to buy *any* fruit that he could. And yet he has returned empty-handed. There is *no* fruit for sale in the market—none! No apples, no pomegranates, no dates, and no persimmons. Not even a single grape!" He threw his hands up into the air.

No fruit for sale? Jasmine thought. How can that be? She knew that hundreds of fruit trees grew in the royal orchards outside Agrabah. Jasmine couldn't remember a time when the palace—and the entire city—was not full of fresh fruit.

Suddenly, Jasmine knew how she wanted to spend the day. She hurried back to the pavilion and placed the bowl of grain near the fountain. Then Abu scampered up to her. He held out his paw for the treat she had promised him.

"I am sorry, Abu," Jasmine said. "There weren't any grapes in the kitchen. Let's go to the market and see if we can find some."

Something strange was happening in the city of Agrabah.

And Jasmine was determined to find out what it was!

Chapter Two

$\mathcal{B}$efore she left the palace, Jasmine changed into a simple brown dress. Then she wrapped a matching plain brown scarf around her head. The scarf hid the bejeweled headband that gave away her royal identity. Jasmine could travel much faster through the crowded streets of Agrabah when people wouldn't be able to recognize her! She grabbed her satchel.

"Ready, Abu?" Jasmine asked as they headed out. Then she laughed as she noticed that Abu had a tiny little satchel of his own. He wore it across his body. "I see, my friend— a place to put your grapes." Jasmine smiled.

Jasmine and Abu left the palace and went through the gate. It was easy to get lost in Agrabah's twisty streets, but Jasmine knew that Abu was a great tour guide! After all, he and Aladdin had lived on the city streets for years before they had come to the palace.

Soon, the pair reached the market. It was one of the busiest and most exciting places in all of Agrabah. Hundreds of stalls and tents lined the streets. Almost anything imaginable was available in the market, from colorful rugs to brass lamps to vivid bolts of fabric. The scents of fragrant spices like cinnamon, cardamom, and coriander filled the air. There were tents that sold silk slippers and leather sandals. There were even tents that sold jewels and gold!

Usually, Jasmine loved to visit each and every stall, admiring all the beautiful and interesting items on display. Today, though, Jasmine and Abu went straight to where they would find fruit.

"Let's start at Mr. Kabali's stand," Jasmine suggested. She had never met Mr. Kabali, but everyone in Agrabah knew that he sold the best apples in town. Jasmine had often heard that the line for Mr. Kabali's fruit stretched all the way down the street.

But today, there was no line at Mr. Kabali's stand.

And there was no fruit!

The baskets on each shelf were empty. Mr. Kabali stood behind the counter, glumly polishing it with a soft cloth.

"Mr. Kabali looks so sad," Jasmine whispered to Abu. "Maybe he knows what happened to the fruit. Let's go talk to him."

"Good morning!" Jasmine called out as she approached. "I was hoping to buy some apples."

Mr. Kabali just shook his head. "I'm very sorry, miss," he replied. "I am afraid I have no apples to offer you."

"Oh, dear," Jasmine said. "Has something happened to the apple harvest?"

Mr. Kabali shrugged his shoulders. "If so, then something has also happened to the date harvest," he replied. "I placed my usual order for two bushels, and yet I received nothing."

"Hopefully things will be right tomorrow," Jasmine said. She smiled encouragingly at Mr. Kabali. He tried to smile back, but Jasmine could tell he was very worried.

Mr. Kabali wasn't the only one. The market was usually full of laughter and chatter as the people of Agrabah visited with their friends and neighbors. But today, everyone seemed quieter than usual as they shopped.

Abu tugged on Jasmine's dress and patted his satchel.

"Of course we'll stop by the grape stand," Jasmine promised him. "But it is all the way across the market. Since the pomegranate stand is closer, let's go there next."

Pomegranates were one of Jasmine's favorite fruits. She loved to drink tall glasses of cool pomegranate juice on hot afternoons.

But to Jasmine's dismay, all the shelves in the pomegranate stand were bare, too.

Then Jasmine and Abu visited the stall that always sold mangoes—well, almost always. Today, the mango stall was closed.

Their next stop was the persimmon seller. Jasmine held her breath as she approached, hoping to see an enormous display of the small orange fruits.

But every basket and shelf was empty.

It was just as the royal chef had said: there wasn't a single piece of fresh fruit for sale in the entire market!

"This is so strange," Jasmine remarked. "Abu, what could have happened?"

There was no reply. Jasmine looked down and realized that the monkey wasn't there!

"Abu?" she said again, louder this time. Jasmine looked to the left and the right. She looked under the counter and on top of the canopy. Abu was nowhere to be seen.

The little monkey was gone!

Chapter Three

"Abu!" Jasmine cried. Her heart started to pound. Even though Abu knew his way around the market, Jasmine was worried that he might have gotten lost. She also knew that sometimes the little monkey took things that didn't belong to him. If Abu got caught stealing, he could be in serious trouble. Jasmine had to find him right away!

Jasmine rushed through the streets of the

marketplace. But soon, she had to stop to rest. She leaned against a tall statue as she tried to catch her breath. If you were Abu, where would *you* go? Jasmine thought to herself.

The princess bit her lip as she tried to answer the question. Then her eyes lit up. "Grapes!" she exclaimed. All day long, Abu had wanted to eat some grapes. Maybe he'd gotten so tired of waiting that he'd wandered off to the grape seller's stand without her!

Jasmine glanced up at the sky. The sun was starting to set, and she didn't want to be out much longer. She had only been to the grape stand once before, but Jasmine was sure she could find it again. It was located across from the high wall that surrounded the city.

Jasmine ran all the way to the southern wall and followed it to the grape stand. By the time she arrived, the market had started to empty. Sellers were packing up their wares and closing their stalls.

"Abu!" Jasmine called again as she approached the grape stand. The last time she'd seen it, dozens of baskets had lined the shelves. Clusters of exotic grapes in every color—red, green, blue, and black—spilled out of the baskets.

But today, the grape stand was empty.

"Oh, Abu, where *are* you?" Jasmine cried.

Suddenly, the monkey jumped out from behind the grape stand and threw his arms around Jasmine's neck.

"Oh!" Jasmine cried, surprised. "Abu, I

was so worried about you! I've been looking for you everywhere!"

Abu started chattering excitedly, jumping up and down as he pointed at the grape stand.

"Yes, yes, I know," Jasmine said. "I am so sorry that there are no grapes. But we must

hurry back to the palace. It will soon be dark!"

Clutching his satchel tightly, Abu rode on Jasmine's shoulder as she ran through the twisting streets of Agrabah. The first stars appeared in the sky just as they reached the palace gates.

"Stop in the name of the Sultan!" Rasoul, the head of the guards, shouted. "Who goes there?"

Jasmine pulled back the scarf to reveal the jewel in her hair. "It is I, Princess Jasmine of Agrabah," she announced.

At once, the guards swung open the heavy metal gates so that the princess could come inside. Abu scurried into the palace.

"There you are," a familiar voice said. Jasmine smiled when she saw who it was.

"I might have known you two were up to something," Aladdin continued with a playful twinkle in his eye as Abu ran past him. "I hope you haven't caused too much trouble today!"

"Well, there *is* trouble," Jasmine said slowly. "But we did nothing to cause it."

A frown crossed Aladdin's face. "You must be tired," he said. "Come, let's sit in the tearoom and you can tell me about it."

On their way into the tearoom, Jasmine and Aladdin passed by the pavilion. "Oh! Look at all the peacocks!" Jasmine cried in delight as six peacocks strutted around the courtyard. She smiled when she saw the Sultan trying to coax one of the birds to eat out of his hand.

"So what happened today?" Aladdin asked when they sat down.

"Something very strange is going on," Jasmine began. She told Aladdin everything, from the missing pancakes at breakfast to the empty fruit stands at the market.

"That *is* strange," Aladdin agreed. "You know, it hasn't rained in a few weeks. Perhaps that has something to do with it."

Jasmine shook her head. "The royal orchards are watered by a series of fountains for precisely that reason. There should be plenty of fruit," she explained. All this talk of water made Jasmine realize that there wasn't any tea on the table! The princess got up to fetch the teapot herself.

"Oh!" she suddenly cried.

"What's wrong?" Aladdin asked, jumping up from his seat.

"I just stepped on something hard," Jasmine told him as she bent down to see what it was. When she picked up the object, she saw that it was a perfect gemstone in the most beautiful shade of purple that she had ever seen.

"It's an amethyst!" Jasmine exclaimed. "But what was it doing on the floor?"

"I have no idea," Aladdin replied. Then he saw something else. "Hey, what's that?" He pointed behind Jasmine. She turned around to see another amethyst glinting on the ground!

"It matches the other one perfectly," Jasmine said. She held the gems up to her

ears. "They would make a lovely pair of earrings, wouldn't they?" She smiled.

Before Aladdin could respond, he and Jasmine heard the sound of something rolling across the floor. They glanced at the doorway just in time to see another amethyst roll to a stop. It sparkled in the light.

Jasmine and Aladdin looked at each other, confused. "These jewels must belong to *someone*," Jasmine said, "and we're going to find out whom!"

Chapter Four

In the corridor outside the tearoom, Jasmine immediately spotted another amethyst.

Then she saw another.

And another!

The precious jewels made a clinking sound as Jasmine clutched them in her hand. Six amethysts . . . then seven . . . then eight . . .

When Jasmine and Aladdin crept around the corner, they found Abu sitting with a pile of amethysts in his lap! Jasmine's hand flew to her mouth as she watched Abu try to bite one of the amethysts. Then he made a face and tossed it away.

"Ow!" Aladdin yelped as the amethyst bounced off his head.

Abu scrambled up, surprised to see Jasmine and Aladdin. He hugged Aladdin's leg tightly and looked up at the prince with his big eyes, clearly upset that he had hurt his friend.

"Okay, okay, okay," Aladdin said with a laugh. "It feels better already. But you've got some explaining to do, Abu. Where did you get these?"

Abu jumped down to the floor and scooped the amethysts together so that

they looked like a bunch of grapes. Then he danced around them, clapping his hands happily.

"So *that's* why you were so excited at the grape stand," Jasmine realized. "You thought you had found some delicious grapes after all."

"I guess these aren't so tasty, are they?" Aladdin joked. "They sure are beautiful, though."

Abu enthusiastically nodded his head in agreement.

"Whoever owns these jewels is probably missing them, don't you think?" Aladdin continued.

Abu stopped to think about it for a moment. Then he nodded his head again.

"Where did you find them, Abu?" Jasmine asked gently. "Were they in the grape stand, or on the street outside it?"

Abu ran over to the wall and started to tap it with his paws.

"By the wall. I understand," Jasmine said. "First thing tomorrow morning, we shall return to the area and look for the amethysts' owner. You can show us exactly where you found them."

Abu helped Jasmine scoop up all the jewels.

"Thank you, Abu," Jasmine told the little monkey. "Now let's get some rest. We've had a long day!"

Early the next morning, Jasmine, Aladdin, and Abu left the palace—and this time, they took the Magic Carpet. Even though the sun had just risen, the market was already bustling with vendors setting up their stalls. As they flew over the market, Jasmine noticed that there still wasn't any fruit among the many items for sale.

When they reached the grape stand, the Magic Carpet landed softly on the ground and the three passengers climbed off. Abu pointed to the area where he had discovered the amethysts.

"Right over there?" Aladdin asked.

Abu nodded.

"Let's ask the vendors if they lost anything yesterday," Jasmine suggested. She approached a tall man. "Excuse me, sir, but we found some valuable property in this area. Did you lose anything recently?"

The man's eyes twinkled greedily. "Like what?" he asked.

"Some purple—" Jasmine began.

But Aladdin quickly cut her off. "Why don't you tell us what you lost, and then we'll tell you if that's what we found," he said.

The man glared at Aladdin.

"Those amethysts are really valuable," Aladdin whispered to Jasmine as he guided her away.

Jasmine smiled at Aladdin, who still knew the streets a little better than she did. He had spent many years on them, after all.

For most of the morning, Jasmine and

Aladdin asked everyone who passed by if they had lost something. But no one had. Abu was ready to give up. He lay down to rest for a moment . . . and fell asleep. Even Jasmine was starting to worry that they wouldn't be able to find the amethysts' owner.

"What happens next?" Jasmine asked Aladdin. "What should we do if we can't return the jewels?"

There was a long pause before Aladdin replied. "Well, we did our best to find the amethysts' owner," he finally said. "Let's go back to the palace and make some signs that we can hang around the marketplace. We can also put the amethysts in the royal vault for safekeeping until their owner comes forward."

"That is an excellent plan," Jasmine said.

She leaned down to wake Abu for the journey back to the palace. But before they left, Jasmine paused. "The royal orchard should be on the other side of this wall. I'd like to take a quick look at it."

"Magic Carpet, can you give Jasmine a boost?" Aladdin asked.

The Magic Carpet shook its tassels happily and folded itself into stairs for Jasmine to climb. Jasmine carefully stepped up so that she could look over the wall.

What she saw was so unexpected that she gasped in surprise!

"What? What is it?" Aladdin asked from the ground.

"I don't think we need to make those signs," Jasmine said. "Look!"

Chapter Five

Jasmine knew she needed to climb down so that Aladdin could look over the wall, too. But she could hardly tear her eyes away from the amazing sight in the orchard. Several times a year, Jasmine and her father visited the orchards as part of their royal duties. But in all those visits, Jasmine had *never* seen anything like this.

The fruit trees were still standing in long

rows that stretched as far as Jasmine could see. There was still an arbor covered in grapevines on the other side of the wall. And each row still contained several tall fountains made from beautiful tiles.

But the trees themselves had changed so much that Jasmine hardly recognized them! They were glittering in the bright sunlight, and Jasmine had to shield her eyes. "It's not possible," she said to Aladdin. "I just don't understand how . . ."

"What is it, Jasmine? What happened?" the prince asked.

"The trees," Jasmine replied. "They are covered in jewels!"

Rubies as big as Jasmine's hand hung from the apple trees. The pomegranates looked like glittering garnets. Gleaming yellow topazes had replaced all the lemons on the lemon trees. And peridot pears hung from the branches of other trees. Even the fountains were filled with glittering sapphires instead of cool, clear water.

Jasmine finally stepped down so that Aladdin could see for himself. He climbed onto the carpet, and his eyes grew wide when he looked over the wall.

"Well, that explains why there hasn't been any fruit in the market," the prince said.

"Let's go," Jasmine responded. She started walking briskly along the wall.

"But Jasmine, the palace is this way," Aladdin called, pointing in the opposite direction.

"Oh, we're not going to the palace," Jasmine replied. "We're going inside the orchard. Follow me!"

"Jasmine, wait a second," Aladdin said as he hurried after her. "Shouldn't we go back to the palace and tell your father?"

"Yes, my father must know about this, and right away," Jasmine agreed. "But he will have just as many questions as we do. I want to bring Ahmed, the orchard keeper, with us. He must know something about what happened to the royal orchards!"

Soon they came to a thick wooden door in the wall. When they stepped through the door into the orchards, Jasmine was once again dazzled by the glittering fruit trees around her. Abu started chattering excitedly as he pointed to the arbor, which was covered with tangles of grapevines. Hundreds of purple amethysts gleamed where the grapes had once grown.

"So this is where the amethysts came from!" Jasmine exclaimed, going over to take a closer look at the clusters of amethysts hanging from the arbor. "I suppose that solves one mystery, doesn't it?"

"But now we have another mystery to figure out," Aladdin said.

Jasmine turned around to see him standing in the doorway of the orchard keeper's hut.

"Where is Ahmed?" Aladdin continued.

"Maybe he's inspecting the trees," Jasmine suggested. She and Aladdin wandered

through the orchard, calling Ahmed's name loudly. Abu followed along for a while but decided to play under the arbor when he got bored. And the Magic Carpet rested inside the hut.

Finally, after searching the entire orchard, Jasmine and Aladdin had to admit that there was no sign of Ahmed anywhere.

Back at the hut, Aladdin had another question. "Why didn't Ahmed come to the palace as soon as this happened?" he asked. "Doesn't he know how serious it is?"

"He must," Jasmine said. "The jewels are stunning to look at, but the people of Agrabah cannot eat jewels. They need fresh, healthy fruit. And the water from the fountains is no use if it's not actually water!

Maybe Ahmed is at the palace right now."

Aladdin shook his head. "I don't think so. His traveling cloak and walking stick are right by the table."

Jasmine glanced over at the table, too. She quickly noticed something else: an unusual-looking pouch made of beautiful blue silk.

"What's this?" Jasmine wondered as she picked up the pouch and carried it outside into the light. Jasmine pulled on a satin cord to open the small pouch. Then she peeked inside.

"How beautiful," she remarked. "Aladdin, what *is* this?"

Aladdin leaned close to the pouch to take a look. The sparkling yellow powder inside it cast a gold light over his face. "I don't know," he admitted. "I don't think I've ever seen anything like it before."

Suddenly, Abu raced out of the arbor. An angry hornet was chasing him!

Abu tore through the orchard, running so fast that he didn't see Jasmine and Aladdin standing outside Ahmed's hut. *Wham!* He knocked into Jasmine, and she stumbled backward before Aladdin steadied her. A tiny bit of the yellow powder spilled onto a wildflower near her feet.

"Abu, be careful!" Aladdin exclaimed.

"Oh, it's all right," she replied, but she was distracted by something on the ground. There, at her feet, was a bright bejeweled wildflower, right where the powder had spilled. Its delicate petals were made of red rubies.

"Aladdin!" Jasmine exclaimed. "It's the powder! The powder must turn things into jewels."

"How is that even possible?" Aladdin marveled.

"I don't know," Jasmine replied. "But I am sure of one thing: it's very dangerous. We have already seen what it did to the royal orchards. Imagine if it spilled in the fields and changed all the vegetables! Look at the fountains—there is not a drop of water to be seen. If this got into Agrabah's water supply, what would we drink?"

"Then it's up to us," Aladdin said firmly. "We must get rid of this immediately . . . before anything else is transformed!"

Chapter Six

$\mathcal{A}$laddin paused for a moment. "But how?"

Jasmine frowned as she closed the silk pouch and tied it shut. "I'm not sure," she admitted. "But we've got to get it as far away from Agrabah as we can."

"That sounds like a job for the Magic Carpet," Aladdin said. He whistled and the carpet jumped up.

"Ready to take a ride?" Aladdin asked.

He held out his hand to help Jasmine climb aboard the hovering carpet. Then Abu scrambled up, too. Jasmine clutched the pouch tightly in both hands as the Magic Carpet soared into the sky.

"Now we just need to figure out where we're going," Aladdin said.

"Let's travel to the desert," Jasmine suggested. "The farther we can get from Agrabah, the better."

"Magic Carpet, can you take us?" Aladdin asked.

The carpet's tassels wagged in agreement. The Magic Carpet picked up speed, traveling so fast that Abu's hat almost blew off! The monkey clasped it with both hands to make sure it stayed on his head.

It didn't take long for the Magic Carpet to zoom across the city limits of Agrabah. The sandy desert stretched as far as Jasmine, Aladdin, and Abu could see. Soon even the beautiful towers of the palace were just a speck in the distance.

"What do you think, Jasmine?" Aladdin asked. "Is this far enough?"

The princess shook her head. "I think we should go just a little farther," she replied. "We can't be too careful with this strange powder."

Jasmine glanced back to see how far they had flown from Agrabah. Suddenly, her eyes opened wide. "Aladdin, look behind you!" she exclaimed.

Aladdin turned around to see another

magic carpet zooming through the sky behind them.

And it was flying faster with every passing second!

Jasmine gasped. "It's Ahmed!" she cried. "I think . . . I think he's following us!"

She and Aladdin watched as the other

carpet flew through the sky at top speed. Soon it was close enough that Jasmine could see the expression on Ahmed's face. His forehead was wrinkled in concentration and he was scowling.

"He looks upset," Aladdin said. "Maybe he knows what we have . . . and maybe he wants it back."

"Faster, Magic Carpet, faster!" Jasmine urged. "Don't let that other carpet catch up with us!"

The Magic Carpet was quick to do as Jasmine said, flying faster than it ever had before.

But that only made the other carpet go faster, too! Soon it was just a few feet behind them.

The Magic Carpet zoomed up so steeply that Jasmine's heart started pounding.

The carpet zipped and zoomed, zigzagging high and low over the desert sands in a desperate attempt to get away from the other flying carpet. But no matter what it tried, Ahmed was right behind them.

"Hold on, everybody!" Aladdin yelled. "We're going for a flip!"

Jasmine grabbed the edge of the Magic Carpet and held on tight. Up, up, up . . . and then *whoosh!* The Magic Carpet turned an upside-down loop.

And as it did, the silk pouch tumbled out of Jasmine's lap!

"Oh, no!" Jasmine cried. She watched as the pouch fell quickly toward the ground.

But it was too late. The pouch had already opened, spilling the sparkling yellow powder all over the desert dunes.

Then, as everyone watched, the few cacti that had sprouted from the sand turned into glimmering objects made of emeralds.

"Whoa!" Aladdin suddenly shouted. "Watch out!"

Jasmine looked away from the glittering cacti just in time to see that the two magic carpets were about to crash! All four of the passengers—Jasmine, Aladdin, Abu, and Ahmed—started to scream as the magic carpets swerved wildly, avoiding each other by inches!

The Magic Carpet had no choice but to make an emergency landing in the middle of the desert. When Jasmine stepped onto the sand, her legs felt very wobbly. Then she burst out laughing. Abu was dazzled by the cacti and he was trying to grab bits of one with his little paws, but it was no use. The emeralds were there to stay.

It was one of the most beautiful sights that Jasmine and Aladdin had ever seen, but they could only enjoy it for a moment. All too soon, they realized that the other flying carpet had been forced to make an emergency landing, too.

And Ahmed was walking right toward them!

Chapter Seven

Jasmine took a deep breath. "We had to destroy the powder, Ahmed," she said in a firm, confident voice. "We had no choice. It was too dangerous to keep within the walls of Agrabah."

Ahmed bowed before her. "Thank you, Princess," he said. When he looked up, his eyes were full of gratitude. "I agree completely!"

Jasmine and Aladdin exchanged a look of relief.

"I was afraid that you didn't know what the powder could do," Ahmed continued. "When I saw you flying away from the orchard, I knew that I had to warn you at once!"

"So *that's* why you were following us," Aladdin said.

"I am so grateful that you have succeeded where I failed. Out here, the powder cannot harm our crops or water," Ahmed told Jasmine and Aladdin.

Jasmine nodded. "And now this beautiful cactus will be a delight for anyone who comes across it in their travels. And it's so sturdy that greedy thieves won't even

be able to take the emeralds!"

"But," Aladdin began, "they *could* take the jeweled fruit in the orchard if they see what it looks like right now."

Jasmine closed her eyes as she imagined what might happen: some people in Agrabah might be so eager to take the jewels that they would pick every bejeweled apple, mango, pomegranate, persimmon, and grape. The orchard would be bare and ruined. We have to get back as soon as we can, Jasmine thought.

Then she turned to Ahmed. "But where did the powder come from?" she asked.

For a moment, Ahmed looked a little embarrassed. Then he started rummaging around in his vest pocket. "A few days ago, I was watering one of the oldest apple trees," he began. "As I shoveled some dirt aside, my shovel struck something hard. I dug around in the soil and found this."

Ahmed handed Jasmine a small silver box that was studded with jewels. Inside the box, Jasmine found a scroll of parchment paper. It was yellowed with age and its edges were tattered. The scroll looked very, very old.

Jasmine unfurled the scroll. Her brow furrowed as she read the words written on it.

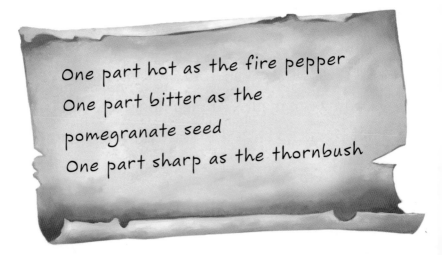

One part hot as the fire pepper
One part bitter as the pomegranate seed
One part sharp as the thornbush

"It looks like . . . some sort of recipe," Jasmine finally said. "But it says nothing about what it actually does."

"I grew very curious, Princess," Ahmed admitted. "So I decided to make the recipe myself. Just for fun. I was very surprised when those ingredients transformed into the yellow powder."

"What made you decide to test it on the orchard?" asked Aladdin.

"No! No! I never wanted that to happen!" Ahmed exclaimed. "You see, as I finished mixing the ingredients, a high wind began," he continued. "I tried to cover the pot as quickly as I could, but it was too late. The wind had already scattered the powder throughout the orchard!"

"I remember that windstorm," Jasmine replied. "It knocked several tiles off the palace roof."

"Oh, Princess, I could hardly believe my eyes," Ahmed said. "I ran from tree to tree in disbelief. Each one had been transformed into a tree of jewels! It was a beautiful sight, but I had no idea how to reverse the spell!"

Jasmine nodded sympathetically. "Come. We will all go back to the orchard and find a way to undo this spell."

Jasmine, Aladdin, Ahmed, and Abu quickly hopped onto their flying carpets. The carpets lifted into the air, soaring through the brilliant blue sky on the way back to Agrabah. When the palace towers finally appeared, Jasmine breathed a sigh of relief.

But she knew there was work to be done.

Aladdin glanced at Jasmine. "You look like you have a plan," he said quietly.

Jasmine shook her head. "Not yet," she whispered back. "But I'm going to come up with one!"

Chapter Eight

$\mathcal{A}$t last, the flying carpets landed in the royal orchard. Jasmine was relieved to see that, apart from some bees buzzing in confusion around the jeweled fruit, the orchard was exactly the same as they had left it. All the sparkling fruit was still on the trees.

"We don't have much time," Jasmine said to the others. "It will not be long before more people come to investigate what has happened to the fruit. We must reverse the spell as quickly as possible. Ahmed, will you take us to the tree where you found the silver box?"

"Right this way, Princess," Ahmed replied.

Ahmed led Jasmine, Aladdin, and Abu through the orchard to the grove of apple trees. The oldest tree of all had thick, gnarled branches and silvery bark.

"Let's keep digging around the tree," Jasmine suggested. "If there is a way to reverse the spell, perhaps it was buried here, too."

Abu went right to work, using his little paws to dig so hard that huge clumps of dirt flew up in the air!

Jasmine started to laugh. "That's the spirit, Abu! We can all help," she said encouragingly.

Jasmine and Aladdin started digging, too—but all they found at the base of the tree were worms and rocks.

Ahmed looked at the trio worriedly. "I fear that digging any deeper would damage the tree's roots," he said.

Aladdin wiped his forehead with his

sleeve. "Phew!" he exclaimed. "That was hard work."

"I suppose if there is a reversal recipe, it could be buried under *any* tree in the orchard," Jasmine remarked.

No one spoke for a long moment. What were they going to do?

"Ahmed, may I see the spell again?" Jasmine asked suddenly.

Ahmed handed the princess the silver box.

Jasmine unfurled the scroll and read the recipe again. "One part hot . . . one part bitter . . . one part sharp," she said slowly. "I think I know what we need to do!"

Everyone—including Abu—looked at her curiously.

"We must write our *own* reversal recipe," Jasmine explained. "Perhaps if we gather the opposite of each ingredient, we will be able to make a powder that reverses the spell!"

"That's a great idea!" Aladdin replied.

"To reverse the recipe, we will need something cold . . . something sweet . . . and something soft," Jasmine told them. "I think we should split up and return to the market. Ahmed, would you find something cold? And Aladdin, if you would find something soft, Abu and I will find something sweet."

"Of course. At your service, Princess," replied Ahmed.

"I'll be back as soon as I can," Aladdin promised.

Abu pulled himself up to his full height

and saluted Jasmine. Together, they slipped through the orchard door so as not to be seen, and started walking briskly through the marketplace. "Something sweet, something sweet, something sweet," Jasmine murmured as they walked. "Honey is sweet, but it's very sticky. I don't think it would mix well with the other ingredients."

Abu started jumping up and down, pointing and chattering. Jasmine saw that they were standing near a stall that sold jams and syrups. "Pomegranate syrup is *very* sweet—but it's also sticky, like honey," Jasmine replied. "As is jam made from dates . . . dates . . . yes! Abu, that's perfect!"

Abu scratched his head and gave Jasmine a questioning look.

"*Sugar* made from dates is sweet and powdery," Jasmine explained as she walked up to the seller. "Excuse me, do you have any date sugar for sale today?"

The seller bowed to the princess. He nodded as he placed a jar of the sugar on the counter. "This is the very last of the date sugar until I can make more, Princess," he said. "And I have not received any deliveries of dates in two days!"

"Hopefully more will be delivered later," Jasmine said quickly. She placed a gold coin in the seller's hand. "Thank you very much!"

Jasmine and Abu ran all the way back to the orchard. Ahmed and Aladdin were waiting for them under the old apple tree.

"You're back!" Aladdin exclaimed. "Look

what I've brought: soft petals from a velvety rose—instead of thorns."

"That's perfect!" cried Jasmine as Aladdin held the delicate petals in his hands. She reached out to touch them.

She turned to Ahmed, who showed her a large scoop of frosty shaved ice in a cold bowl.

"Wonderful," Jasmine said. "Abu and I were successful in the market, too. We have brought some date sugar."

No one spoke as Jasmine poured everything into the pot.

Then the orchard keeper gave Jasmine a long silver spoon. "Princess, would you like to combine the ingredients?" he asked.

Jasmine smiled at him as she took the

spoon and started to stir everything. The ingredients swirled together. The ice melted, and soon there was a shimmering purple powder in the pot.

Ahmed nodded. "This is what happened before. But the powder was yellow, not purple."

"I know," Jasmine said. She bit her lip in concern. "I hope the change in color means that we have reversed the recipe."

As Jasmine stared into the pot, she knew that they would find out soon!

Chapter Nine

"You know, we have no idea what this powder does," Aladdin pointed out. "I think we should test it on one apple before we spread it through the whole orchard."

"That's a good idea," Ahmed told him.

As Jasmine finished stirring all the ingredients together, a gentle breeze ruffled her hair. The breeze grew stronger and stronger. "Oh! The purple powder!" Jasmine cried. She tried to cover the pot, but it was too late. A ferocious gust of wind swirled around her, lifting the powder right out of the pot and blowing it around the orchard!

The wind was so fierce that Jasmine, Aladdin, Ahmed, and Abu had to cover their faces and close their eyes. It even made the heavy jeweled fruit on the trees start clacking together noisily, drowning out all other sounds.

Then, just as quickly as it had started, the sudden wind died down. The orchard was quiet and still.

Jasmine took a deep breath. Then she opened her eyes, hardly daring to imagine what she might see around her.

The trees were standing as tall and

solid as always. Soft green leaves fluttered on every tree. But best of all—none of the fruit was sparkling! Apples and pomegranates, dates and persimmons, lemons, mangoes, and pears filled the heavy branches. Their sweet fragrance perfumed the entire orchard.

"It worked!" Jasmine cried, shocked. "It really worked! We reversed the spell!"

"Well done, Princess," Ahmed said as a broad smile crossed his face.

"The reversal recipe was a great idea," Aladdin agreed.

"What do you say, Abu?" Jasmine asked playfully. "Are you ready for some grapes?"

But there was no answer.

"Abu?" Aladdin called. "Where did you go, you little rascal?"

Jasmine smiled. "I think I know," she said.

Aladdin and Ahmed followed Jasmine over to the grape arbor. They found Abu sprawled out beneath the vines, smacking his lips happily as he ate one juicy grape after another.

"I don't blame you, Abu," Jasmine said, laughing. "You have waited a long time for those grapes!" Then her hands flew up to her mouth. "Oh! I almost forgot!"

Jasmine ran over to where she had left her bag. She came back with the handful of amethysts that Abu had mistaken for grapes. "I suppose they didn't transform because they were inside my bag," she said as she offered the amethysts to Ahmed. "These belong to you. Abu found them outside the orchard wall."

Ahmed shook his head. "No, Princess, I wouldn't dream of it," he replied. "I give them to you as a token of my deep appreciation. Thank you for helping me reverse the spell and restore the fruit."

"Are you sure?" Jasmine asked.

"Yes," Ahmed said firmly. "You must take them back to the palace with you."

"Thank you, Ahmed," Jasmine replied, smiling. "I will treasure them always. And— if it's quite all right with you—"

"Yes, Princess?" Ahmed asked.

"I would like to bring back some dates and apples for my father's breakfast tomorrow," she finished.

"And so you shall!" Ahmed announced. "I will pick the finest dates and apples in the orchard for His Majesty, the Sultan!"

The next morning, Jasmine woke excitedly. She, Aladdin, and Abu had arrived home late the night before and Jasmine had gone immediately to one of her favorite people—the royal jeweler. When Jasmine had finished getting dressed in the morning, she hurried to the dining room. She couldn't wait to show Aladdin the shimmering earrings that the jeweler had made for her using the amethysts . . . and she couldn't wait to see her father's face when Rajeed served him a tall stack of date-and-apple pancakes!

"Good morning, everyone," Jasmine said as she sat down at the table.

"Good morning, dear!" the Sultan replied, beaming at his daughter. "You are looking especially lovely this fine day. Are those new earrings?"

Jasmine caught Aladdin's eye. "Yes, Father, they are," she said.

"They're almost as beautiful as you are," Aladdin said, smiling at her.

Rajeed was in a good mood, too, as he placed an enormous silver platter next to the Sultan's plate and removed the cover with a flourish. Everyone gasped to see a giant pile of pancakes full of sweet dates and juicy apples. "Oh, splendid!" cried the Sultan. "This is just what I wanted for breakfast!"

"Breakfast? Did somebody say breakfast?" a familiar voice yelled through the window.

It was the Genie!

"Welcome, Genie!" Aladdin exclaimed. "When did you get here?"

"I just flew in, and boy, are my arms tired," the Genie joked, flapping his arms as he sailed into the room. "I passed the pavilion on the way—those peacocks sure are beautiful. So, did I miss anything exciting?"

Jasmine and Aladdin smiled and exchanged a knowing look.

"Ooh, what do we have here?" the Genie said excitedly, forgetting what he had asked. "Date-and-apple pancakes? My favorite! Oh, you shouldn't have, but since you did, don't mind if I do!"

The Genie grabbed a large batch of pancakes off the serving platter. Then he winked at Abu and started to juggle them!

"How about *that* for some early morning entertainment?" he joked.

Abu reached up to try to grab a pancake. He was hungry, as usual!

After a few moments, the Genie put the pancakes back. Then he proceeded to serve the Sultan, Jasmine, Aladdin, and even Abu

their pancakes! He poured syrup onto their plates and pulled up a chair.

"Let's eat!" he announced.

Jasmine smiled and took a big bite of a pancake. It was delicious. And in addition to the Sultan's favorite pancakes, there was also tons of fresh fruit as breakfast choices. There was a persimmon salad, fresh sparkling pomegranate juice, and bowls and platters of ripe fruit.

It may not have been as beautiful as a table full of sparkling jewels, but to Jasmine, it was even better than that. She knew the city of Agrabah would be safe and happy now that things were back to normal!

Disney
PRINCESS

Collect all the books in this exciting new series of
original stories—each starring a Disney Princess!

Ariel
The Shimmering Star Necklace

Cinderella
The Lost Tiara

Belle
The Charming Gift

Jasmine
The Jewel Orchard

Sparkly
Covers!

Disney makes
reading royally fun

Available wherever books are so

Disney PRESS
disneybooks.com